Dear Parents:

Congratulations! Your child is taking the first steps on an exciting journey. The destination? Independent reading!

STEP INTO READING® will help your child get there. The program offers five steps to reading success. Each step includes fun stories and colorful art or photographs. In addition to original fiction and books with favorite characters, there are Step into Reading Non-Fiction Readers, Phonics Readers and Boxed Sets, Sticker Readers, and Comic Readers—a complete literacy program with something to interest every child.

Learning to Read, Step by Step!

Ready to Read   Preschool–Kindergarten
• big type and easy words • rhyme and rhythm • picture clues
For children who know the alphabet and are eager to begin reading.

Reading with Help   Preschool–Grade 1
• basic vocabulary • short sentences • simple stories
For children who recognize familiar words and sound out new words with help.

Reading on Your Own   Grades 1–3
• engaging characters • easy-to-follow plots • popular topics
For children who are ready to read on their own.

Reading Paragraphs   Grades 2–3
• challenging vocabulary • short paragraphs • exciting stories
For newly independent readers who read simple sentences with confidence.

Ready for Chapters   Grades 2–4
• chapters • longer paragraphs • full-color art
For children who want to take the plunge into chapter books but still like colorful pictures.

STEP INTO READING® is designed to give every child a successful reading experience. The grade levels are only guides; children will progress through the steps at their own speed, developing confidence in their reading. The F&P Text Level on the back cover serves as another tool to help you choose the right book for your child.

Remember, a lifetime love of reading starts with a single step!

For Wesley
—M.F.

All rights reserved. Published in the United States by Random House Children's Books,
a division of Penguin Random House LLC, New York. Originally published in a different form
by Random House Children's Books as a Pictureback® Book in 1990 and as a Jellybean Book™ in
1998.

Step into Reading, Random House, and the Random House colophon are registered trademarks of
Penguin Random House LLC.

Visit us on the Web!
StepIntoReading.com
randomhousekids.com

Educators and librarians, for a variety of teaching tools, visit us at RHTeachersLibrarians.com

Library of Congress Cataloging-in-Publication Data
Names: Herman, Gail, author. | Fleming, Michael, illustrator.
Title: Time for school, little dinosaur / by Gail Herman, Michael Fleming.
Description: First Edition. | New York : Random House, [2017] | Series: Step into reading.
Step 1 | Summary: Though his friend Spikey teases him, Little Dinosaur is eager to be ready
for his first day of school.
Identifiers: LCCN 2016039897 | ISBN 978-0-399-55645-6 (paperback) |
ISBN 978-0-399-55646-3 (GLB) | ISBN 978-0-399-55647-0 (ebook)
Subjects: | CYAC: First day of school—Fiction. | Dinosaurs—Fiction. | BISAC: JUVENILE
FICTION / Animals / Dinosaurs & Prehistoric Creatures. | JUVENILE FICTION / Stories in
Verse. | JUVENILE FICTION / School & Education.
Classification: LCC PZ7.H4315 Ti 2017 | DDC [E]—dc23

Printed in the United States of America
10 9 8 7 6 5 4 3 2 1

This book has been officially leveled by using the F&P Text Level Gradient™ Leveling System.

Time for School, Little Dinosaur

WITHDRAWN

by Gail Herman

illustrated by Michael Fleming

Random House 🏠 New York

Little Dinosaur
wakes up.

4

He packs his
book bag.

He packs his
lunch box.
He is getting
ready for school.

"Little Dinosaur,"
says Spikey,
"it is summer.
There is no school."

"I am getting ready,"
says Little Dinosaur.
"I am getting ready
for school."

Each day,
Little Dinosaur
wakes up.

He packs his
book bag.

He packs his
lunch box.

He waits for
the school bus.

15

Each day,
Spikey wakes up.

"It is summer," he says.
"Little Dinosaur
    is getting ready.
    But not me!"

It is time for school.
Little Dinosaur
wakes up.

He is ready!

Spikey wakes up.

Oh, no!
His book bag
is not ready!

21

Oh, no!
His lunch box
is not ready!
Will he be late?

Little Dinosaur
waits for the bus.
He waits at the
bus stop.

24

Here is the bus.

Where is Spikey?

"Wait,"

says Little Dinosaur.

"Wait for Spikey!"

SCHOOL BUS

"Here I am,"
says Spikey.

"I was not ready.
But tomorrow I will be!
Just like you,
Little Dinosaur."

And he is!